GET MORE FROM THE STORY!

What color would you make Alfred?
Download FREE coloring and activity pages
at the link below!

www.brandoncullum.com/ALFRED

This book is dedicated to the 216 people who helped tell Alfred's first story.

ISBN: 1517403138
ISBN 13: 978-1517403133

ALFRED

THE TIME TRAVELING

DINOSAUR

Brandon CULLUM and Friends

There once was a dinosaur named Alfred.
He was scary and mean, the other dinosaurs said.
He would roam around the land,
Looking for someone to play
A very special game he was playing that very day.

In the distance
He saw the Triceratops named Tri.
He snuck up behind her,
Hiding beside a bush nearby.

ROAR!!!

Alfred yelled with all of his might.

Terrified, Tri ran
Until she was out of sight.

Rolling on the ground,
Alfred laughed with joy.
He had been playing this game
Since he was a little boy

Rain or shine,
Sleet or snow,
Alfred would play with every single dinosaur
He had come to know.

It was the very next day
And Alfred was ready to play.
Vinny the Velociraptor
Headed Alfred's way.

Alfred took a deep breath,
With all of his might.
"This will be a great scare," thought Alfred,
"I will give him a great fright."

As Alfred got ready to let out his mighty roar,
His tail raised higher and higher
Until he couldn't move it any more.

Above branch one and close to branch three,
Alfred's tail had gotten stuck
On top of a tree!

Alfred yelled, "I'm stuck in a tree!
My tail won't move, I can't get free!"

Vinny took one look,
But didn't stop.
He knew who Alfred was,
And a friend he was not.

"No one likes you," Vinny said,
"No one likes you at all.
Everyday you scare us,
Whether we are tiny or tall."

"I hope you get help,"
Vinny said as he walked away.
"But not from me
and not today."

Alfred pulled as tears filled his eyes.
His tail wouldn't budge, and he began to cry.
With one last pull there was a crack at the top.

"I don't have any friends," thought Alfred,
And then a loud....

POP!

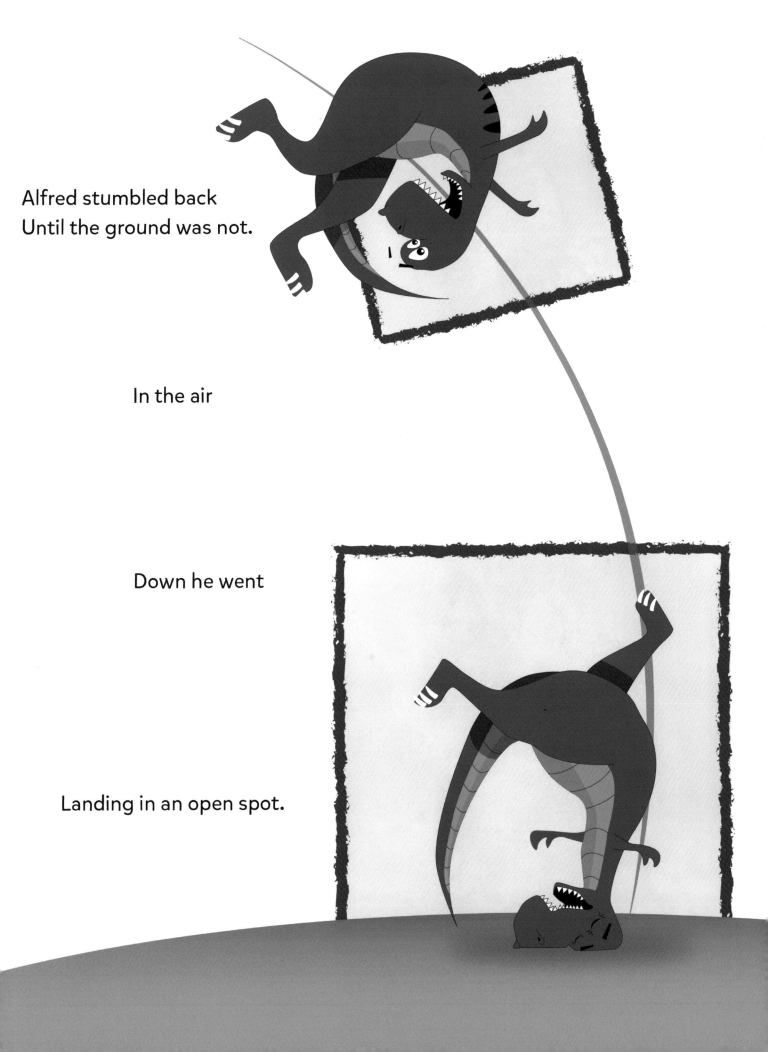

Alfred stumbled back
Until the ground was not.

In the air

Down he went

Landing in an open spot.

"Where am I," thought Alfred,
"Where could I be?"
Then he saw it in the distance,
A huge glowing tree.

Alfred took one step inside
And everything went

BLACK!

Alfred stepped into the light and couldn't believe what he saw!
Dinosaurs everywhere, and they weren't running at all!
Alfred ran to the one that was closest to him.
"Hi," Alfred said,
"Is your name Tim?"

But Tim didn't move,
He stared straight ahead.
"Hey," Alfred got louder,
"Why are you ignoring me?"
Alfred said.

Alfred went to all the other dinosaurs,
But they were exactly the same.
"What is going on?" Alfred asked.
"I don't even know your name."

HEY!

Someone shouted across the way.
"This exhibit is lame,
This is a waste of our day!"

Alfred looked into the distance
And couldn't believe what he saw.
There stood the strangest looking dinosaur
Standing only 5 feet 2 inches tall.

His name was Diesel, and he quickly came near.
"This one looks like a toy," he said with a sneer.

Alfred shot across the room
As fast as his legs would go.

He roared and showed his teeth.
They were as white as snow.

The little dinosaur blinked:

one
two
three
four.

Then he sneered and said,
"Told you he was fake.
Come on, where's the door?"

Again and again,
strange little dinosaurs came inside.
Again and again they laughed,
And Alfred began to cry.

haha!

HaHaHa!

HAha!

"No one likes me," he said,
"Not a single one."
"I'm leaving this place,
back to where I'm from."

Alfred turned to face the strange glowing tree.
Except it was gone from the place it should be.

In the distance was another light
That he walked through.
Little did Alfred know,
He had just entered the New York City Zoo.

Alfred ran as fast as he could.

Terrified! Hiding behind bushes along the way.

He dodged people, then cars, then a taxi.

Hiding behind a window, called "Sorbet."

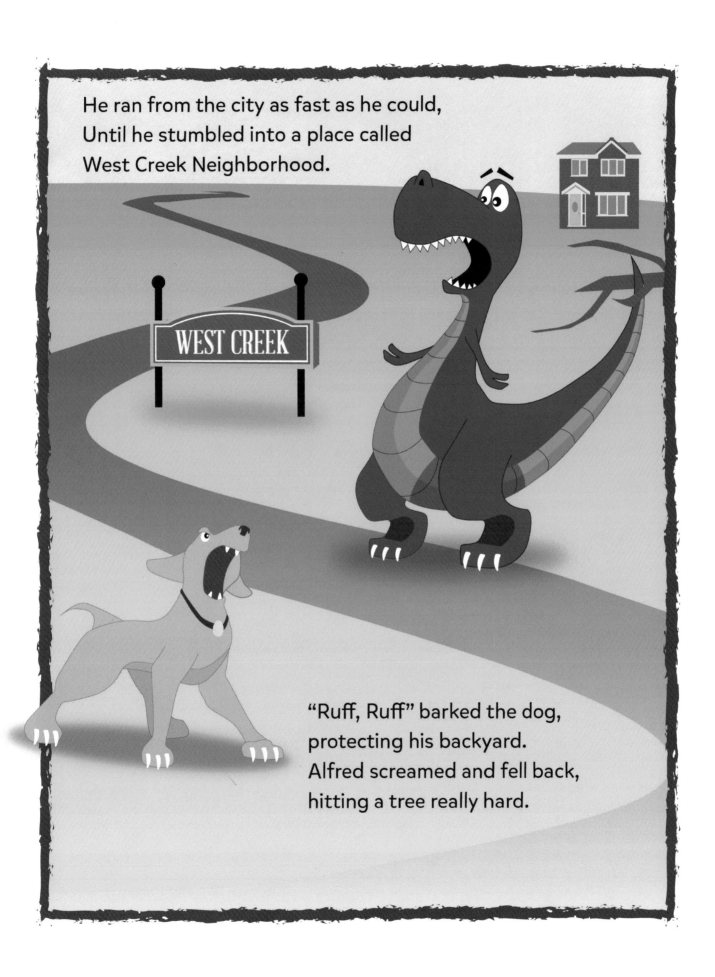

He ran from the city as fast as he could,
Until he stumbled into a place called
West Creek Neighborhood.

WEST CREEK

"Ruff, Ruff" barked the dog,
protecting his backyard.
Alfred screamed and fell back,
hitting a tree really hard.

"Who is there?" said a little girl.
"Who could it be?
Why don't you come out from that great big tree?"

Alfred couldn't move, he was stuck once again.
The little girl grabbed a rope and counted...

One, two, three, four....... TEN!

Alfred's tail was free,
But he wasnt sure what to do.
"Is she going to laugh at me,
Like all the other ones too?"

The girl reached out her hand,
waiting for Alfred to respond.
"My name is Chloe,
And I'm pretty strong!"

Alfred leaned his head
In and then down.
Finally, a friend he had found!

Alfred and Chloe
Became the best of friends

He would help her see really far

She would help him write with pens

Alfred finally learned the secret
That all real friends find true.

Games are a lot more fun
If they aren't just for one, but for two.

One day Chloe asked how Alfred would get back.
Alfred stood for a minute, not sure what to do.
Then he pointed towards the big city
And the New York City Zoo.

"We will have a great adventure," said Chloe.
"We are the best of friends,
the best there could ever be."

Alfred nodded and thought,
"We sure are,
Let's just stay away from the trees."

ALFRED NEEDS YOUR HELP!

Will Alfred ever make it back home?
YOU get to help decide.

Vote on all sorts of things that will be apart of
Book TWO in the Alfred series!

Sign up at the link below and
Join Alfred's next adventure!

www.brandoncullum.com/ALFREDTWO